Enjoy your new life,
enjoy your family.

Thx for every think it was a
pleasure to work with you.
Cristina

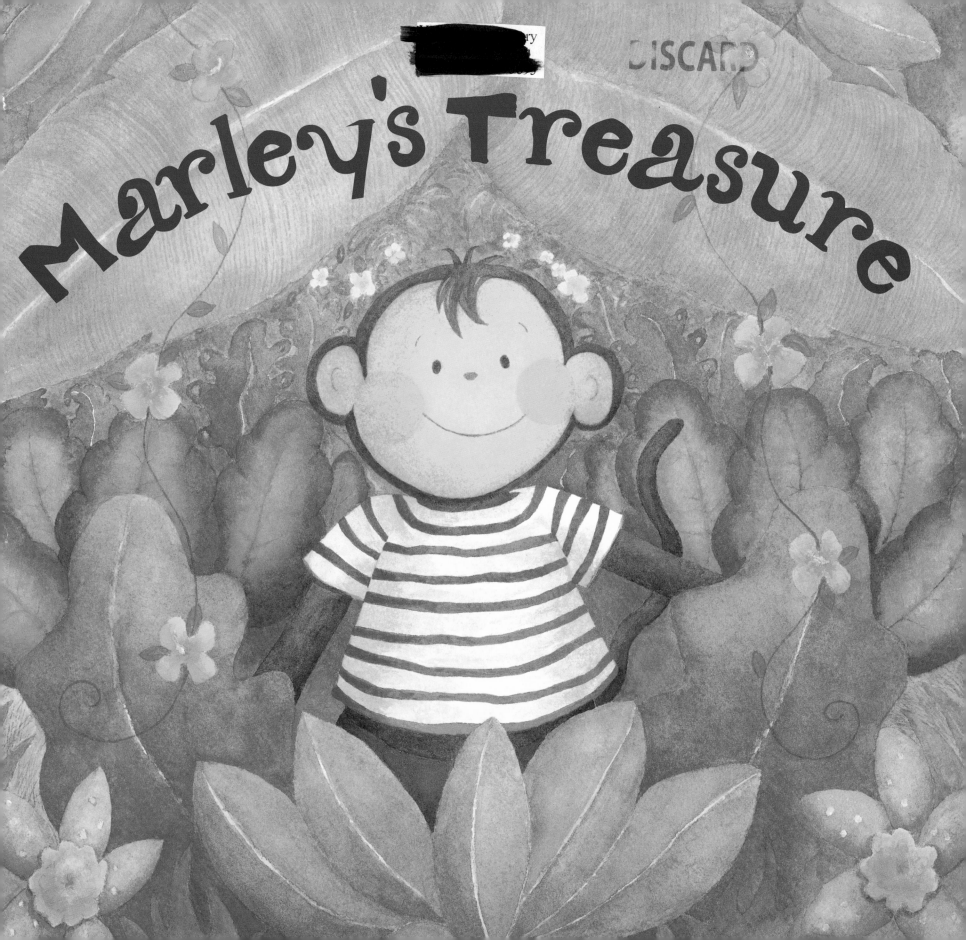

Marley's Treasure

DEDICATION

I wrote this book for my little brother, Mason. I wanted him to know how important
it is to understand the value of friends and family, and that you should always be yourself.
I hope he will also learn not to be selfish and how awfully good it feels to share and give to others.

I want to give special thanks to my mom and dad – they've always been there for me no matter what,
and have truly taught me the value of life, friends and family. I hope you enjoy the story.

– Gabe

For my favorite little monkeys – Lily, Miles and Holden.

– Jennifer

YORKVILLE PRESS
NEW YORK, NEW YORK

Text ©2006 Gable Yerrid
Illustrations ©2006 Jennifer Fitzgerald
Cover illustration ©2006 Jennifer Fitzgerald

For information regarding permission contact:
Yorkville Press, 1202 Lexington Avenue #315, New York, New York 10028

Library of Congress Cataloging-in-Publication Data

Yerrid, Gable.
  Marley's treasure / by Gable Yerrid ; illustrations by Jennifer
Fitzgerald.
      p. cm.
  Summary: Marley the monkey lives a happy life on a beautiful island
with his friends until he discovers some golden bananas and his attitude
toward life changes for the worse.
  ISBN 978-0-9767442-6-9 (alk. paper)
  [1. Monkeys--Fiction. 2. Generosity--Fiction. 3. Sharing--Fiction.] I.

Fitzgerald, Jennifer, 1964- ill. II. Title.
  PZ7.Y495Mar 2007
  [E]--dc22

                              2007003911

Printed in the USA
10 9 8 7 6 5 4 3 2 1

Marley's Treasure

By Gable Yerrid
Illustrations by Jennifer Fitzgerald

YORKVILLE
PRESS

A long time ago, on an island far, far away, there lived a monkey named Marley. Marley lived in a bamboo hut in the oldest tree on the island. From this tree he could see his entire world. Marley loved his life on the island and would not change a thing.

One beautiful morning, Marley decided to lie in his hammock and watch the sunrise while he sipped on a cool cup of coconut milk. As he lay there, he closed his eyes and listened to the sounds of his world. He listened to the wind blowing through the trees, the birds singing their morning songs, and felt the cool breeze that came off the blue water as it brushed against his face. He was happy.

Just then, as the sun came over the horizon, Marley noticed a glow coming from the trees on the far side of the island. He had never seen anything like this before and was so curious, he put down his drink and slid down the tree in a hurry. As soon as his feet hit the ground, he dropped to all fours and ran as fast as he could toward the glowing trees.

Marley tore through the jungle, jumping and swinging from vine to vine. He knew

there was something special happening in his life. As he got closer, the light grew brighter.

He glided through the large green tree leaves and bushes that seemed to grow thicker

as he pushed forward.

And there, hanging from a tree, was a bunch of the most beautiful golden bananas

he'd ever seen - so golden that they glowed like the sun.

"Treasure!" thought Marley. "A beautiful treasure I have dreamed about all my life!"

Marley scurried up the tree and snatched the whole beautiful bunch. Then he fell to the ground, never letting go. He lay there all day hugging the magnificent golden bananas.

Finally, Marley got up, strapped the glowing treasure onto his back, and ran as fast as he could to his bamboo hut. He hoped that no one had seen him find the precious treasure. It was his and his alone. Nervous and afraid, he locked the golden bananas in a chest and stayed in his hut to guard them for six days in a row. He did not sleep. He did not eat. The golden bananas were all that mattered.

When nobody had seen Marley for a week, talk began to spread around the island. Marley's friends were worried and decided to go visit him. What had happened to their friend, they wondered - where had he gone? What had he found?

One day, Lester the turtle showed up at the base of Marley's tree and yelled for Marley to come down. Marley recognized his friend's voice, but was afraid that Lester might have seen him take the golden bananas. Marley slowly walked outside and leaned over the porch towards Lester.

"Oh, ummm, hey Lester," said Marley in a timid voice.

"Hi, Marley!" said Lester. "Long time, no see. What've you been up to lately?"

"Up to? Nothing! Why? Did you hear something? Because whatever you heard, it's not true!"

Lester looked at Marley with a confused expression, turned around and walked away. Marley didn't care. He ran back inside to guard his treasure. After all, he had the golden bananas and nothing else mattered anymore.

The next day, Marley walked outside his hut to find his friend Putter the seagull

sitting on the porch waiting for him.

"WHAT ARE YOU DOING HERE?" Marley screamed. "GO AWAY!

I DON'T HAVE ANYTHING!"

Putter was scared. He had known Marley his entire life and he had never

seen him act this way. He flew off as fast as his wings could carry him.

Eventually, word got around the island that Marley was acting very strangely,

staying in his hut all the time and attacking anyone who came near.

Marley's friends no longer came to see him, and he began to feel lonely. He was

becoming more and more sad every day, but there was no way he was going

to give up his treasure. After all, he was rich and no longer needed friends or

anyone else. Then one day, the great pelican Pete came to visit him.

Pete had lived on the island longer than anyone could remember. He was very old and very wise. He explained to Marley that being alone could really bring him down and that being greedy affected everyone, and everything, around him. Pete explained the real treasure of life was not found in a bunch of golden bananas.

Marley was sad. Pete told him that the other animals were feeling sad, too. He encouraged Marley to share his treasure, to talk to his friends. Then with a SWOOSH he was gone.

Marley sat and thought about what Pete had said. He realized what he had become and he did not like it one bit. Suddenly, he knew there was a solution to his unhappiness. He decided to give the shining golden bananas away.

Jumping up, he grabbed the bananas and ran through the jungle, giving his treasure to those who needed it. One by one he found his friends and told them what had happened and how sorry he was. He shared his shining treasure, and each time he gave a golden banana away he felt better.

Magically, Marley began to feel a glow within his chest. His friends could see the difference as happiness returned to Marley's heart.

That night, Marley threw a big party on the beach for all of his friends. There was music and dancing and a lot of laughter. Marley was happy to be surrounded by friends again.

After the party, when all the guests had gone, Marley sat on the sand with a huge grin on his face. He felt even better than he did when he first saw the golden bananas. Friendship and happiness - that was what meant the most to Marley now. And at that moment under the stars, although he didn't realize it, Marley discovered the most valuable treasure of all... giving was so much better than getting!

Life was good again and Marley realized that the treasures of life he had found would never be lost, as long as he shared with others.

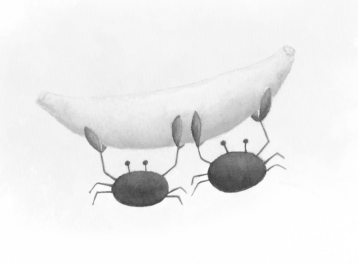